Note to parents, carers and teachers

Read it yourself is a series of modern stories, favourite characters, traditional tales and first reference books written in a simple way for children who are learning to read. The books can be read independently or as part of a guided reading session.

Each book is carefully structured to include many high-frequency words vital for first reading. The sentences on each page are supported closely by pictures to help with understanding, and to offer lively details to talk about.

The books are graded into four levels that progressively introduce wider vocabulary and longer text as a reader's ability and confidence grows.

Ideas for use

- Begin by looking through the book and talking about the pictures. Has your child heard this story or looked at this subject before?

- Help your child with any words he does not know, either by helping him to sound them out or supplying them yourself.

- Developing readers can be concentrating so hard on the words that they sometimes don't fully grasp the meaning of what they're reading. Answering the quiz questions at the end of the book will help with understanding.

For more information and advice on Read it yourself and book banding, visit www.ladybird.com/readityourself

Book Band
6

Level 2 is ideal for children who have received some reading instruction and can read short, simple sentences with help.

Special features:

Frequent repetition of subject words and concepts

Short, simple sentences

Careful match between text and pictures

Large, clear labels and captions

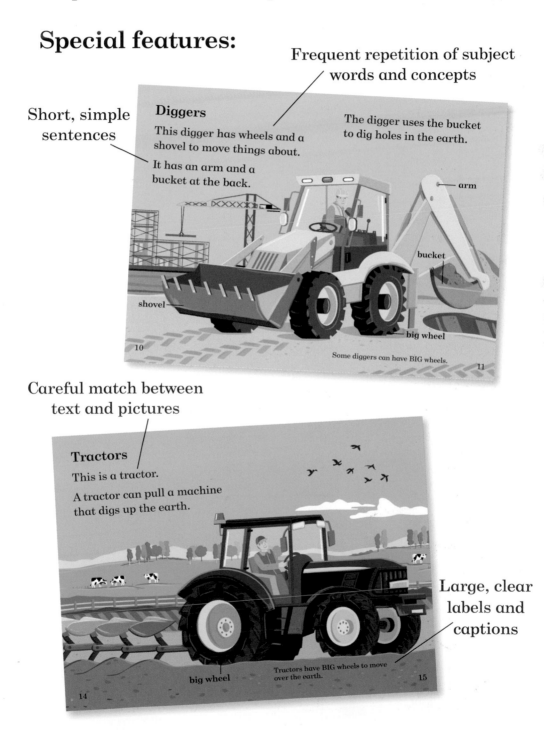

Diggers

This digger has wheels and a shovel to move things about.

It has an arm and a bucket at the back.

The digger uses the bucket to dig holes in the earth.

arm

bucket

shovel

big wheel

10

Some diggers can have BIG wheels.

11

Tractors

This is a tractor.

A tractor can pull a machine that digs up the earth.

big wheel

Tractors have BIG wheels to move over the earth.

14

15

Educational Consultant: Geraldine Taylor
Book Banding Consultant: Kate Ruttle
Subject Consultant: Jason Walker

LADYBIRD BOOKS

UK | USA | Canada | Ireland | Australia
India | New Zealand | South Africa

Ladybird Books is part of the Penguin Random House group of companies
whose addresses can be found at global.penguinrandomhouse.com.

ladybird.com

Penguin
Random House
UK

First published 2015
001

Printed in China

A CIP catalogue record for this book is available from the British Library

ISBN: 978-0-723-29508-2

Big Machines

Written by Monica Hughes
Illustrated by Jenna Riggs

Contents

Machines that help

Big machines help people to dig holes in the earth. Big machines help us to lift things, move things, push and pull things.

Machines help people.

digger

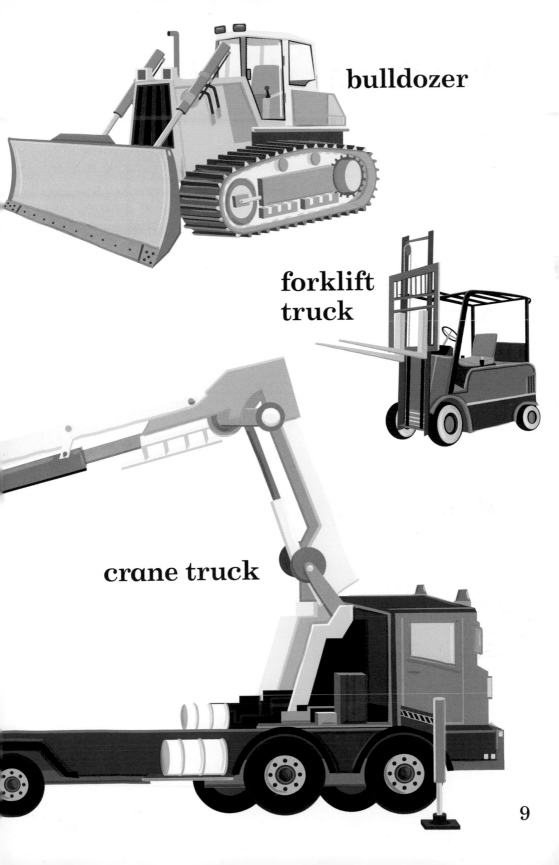

bulldozer

forklift
truck

crane truck

9

Diggers

This digger has wheels and a shovel to move things about.

It has an arm and a bucket at the back.

shovel ——

The digger uses the bucket to dig holes in the earth.

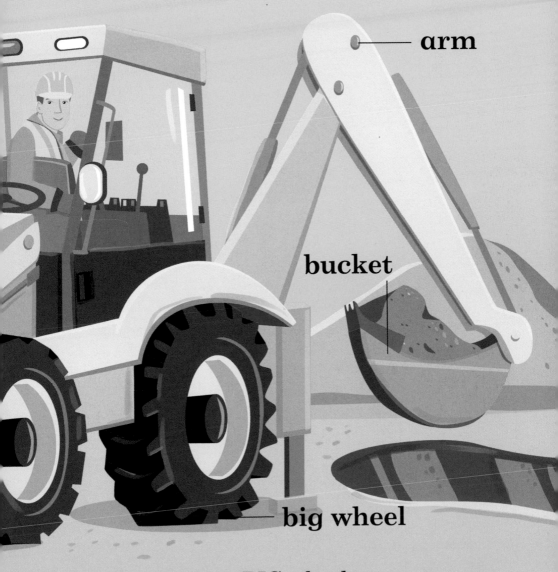

arm

bucket

big wheel

Some diggers have BIG wheels.

Diggers with tracks

Here is another digger.
It has tracks, not wheels,
to move over the earth.

It has a big arm and
a big bucket.

bucket

Some diggers use tracks to
move over the earth.

arm

tracks

13

Tractors

This is a tractor.

A tractor can pull a machine that digs up the earth.

big wheel

Tractors have BIG wheels to move over the earth.

Trucks

Here is a truck that can move things about.

The back of the truck can go up and down.

Trucks can move things about.

Crane trucks

Here is another truck.
It has a crane on the back
that can go up and down.

The crane can lift things
up and move them about.

——— **crane**

A crane truck can lift BIG things.

Forklift trucks

This is a forklift truck.
It uses forks to lift things
up and move them about.

forks

A forklift truck can move BIG things about.

Concrete mixers

Here is a concrete mixer.
It has concrete in the back
that can go into holes.

concrete

hole

The concrete is in the hole.

Wheel loaders

This is a wheel loader. It has a shovel on it that can go up and down.

The shovel can lift things up and move them out of the way.

shovel ——

The wheel loader has a BIG shovel.

Bulldozers

This is a bulldozer.
It has a blade on it.
The blade can go up and
down, and push things out
of the way.

arm

blade

The bulldozer has tracks, not wheels.

tracks

The bulldozer has a BIG blade to push big things out of the way.

Picture glossary

 arm

 blade

 bucket

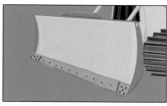 bulldozer

 concrete mixer

 crane truck

 digger

 forklift truck

 shovel

 tracks

 tractor

 wheel loader

Index

Big machines quiz

What have you learnt about big machines? Answer these questions and find out!

- What does a digger use its bucket to do?

- What does a crane truck do?

- Which machines have tracks, not wheels?

- Which truck has a blade at the front?

Tick the books you've read!

Level 2

Level 3

The Read it yourself with Ladybird
app is now available